THE LAST ONE GIRL

ADAM JAMES

Made with ♥ on the Notion Press Platform
www.notionpress.com

To, the many people who inspired me.

Contents

Preface   *vii*

  1. The Diary   1

  2. The Forgotten Past   14

  3. Early Days   34

  4. No One Is Worth It!   42

  5. The Last Fall   58

Preface

Welcome to "The Last One Girl," a journey through the intricate labyrinth of human emotions and the twists of fate that shape our lives. This book draws inspiration from my personal diary entries, reflecting my deepest thoughts, experiences, and the complex emotions that have colored my world.

In these pages, you will find stories of love, loss, friendship, and the pursuit of dreams. Each entry is a piece of my soul, laid bare for you to see. The characters you will meet are fragments of my reality, each one representing a part of me and the people who have touched my life.

As you read, I hope you find a connection to your own experiences and emotions. My goal is to take you on a journey where you can feel, reflect, and perhaps see the world a little differently through the lens of these entries.

Thank you for joining me on this personal journey. I hope "The Last One Girl" resonates with you and offers a glimpse into the beauty and complexity of our shared human experience.

ONE
THE DIARY

It all started when I found myself wandering around my friend's room like a nocturnal bird. As a child, I was always captivated by the book collections and study areas that my friends had. Their books and belongings fascinated me, and this curiosity felt like a wonder of heaven, even now. I took the opportunity to look around while my friend was away.

His bookshelf, covered in dust, suggested it hadn't been touched or cleaned in a long time. I perused the first shelf, mentally noting which books I had already seen. When I moved to the second shelf, I discovered a collection of books I hadn't encountered before. As a teenager, I was deeply drawn to the overwhelming curiosity and fascination these books inspired. I often believed that the only way to make a significant impact on the world was to achieve something far greater than the ordinary purposes of living. I dreamed of discoveries that would define the existence of the universe and prove the reality of the multiverse and other beings like us.

However, life must be lived realistically. You need to accept your weaknesses and work on what you can improve. These are the things that make us human, setting us apart from all other species on Earth. We never settle for less; we always strive for more and often achieve it. But enough of this philosophical musing.

Returning to the shelf, I found something very interesting: a book with yellowed pages and an elegant black cover. It seemed personal, and I hesitated to look inside. But my curiosity got the better of me, urged on by the devilish voice of temptation. "Damn you, Lucifer," I thought. First, I locked the door. Then, I opened the book—my friend Adam's golden work of art.

To my surprise, the first page began with "Dear Bro." For a moment, I didn't realize that Adam had been writing a diary addressed to his brother. But wait, he didn't have a brother. Maybe a cousin? No, I guessed not. I decided to let it go.

"*16th August, 2014*

Dear Bro,

Talking with my only friend, the one I could confide in about anything, no matter how it might be received. He never got bored with what I shared or felt any of the emotions I experienced. He was as blank as an empty cup, ready to be filled endlessly with my thoughts, emotions, and stories. He never pried into my life or asked for anything he shouldn't know. He remained silent, waiting for someone to take him in their hands, to touch his soft pages and breathe in his ambrosial scent.

This friend of mine was always available, day or night, 24/7, 365 days a year. Year after year, he journeyed with me, until he was full and needed one of his cousins or offspring to continue the journey. But that didn't mean he was forgotten. He remained in my heart, ready to reflect back the immense experiences and feelings from the times I had confided in him.

He was the friend of everyone: the blank white pages protected by a hard cover to safeguard the precious information inside. His name was Alex. I hated calling him a notebook because he was more than that. He embodied the essence of a true friend. He listened to everything I had to say and helped me find solutions to my problems.

Yours,
Adam James **"**

Reading this, I thought, "What the heck? Adam might be this kind of guy inside?" I never imagined something deeper was going on in his world of misery and chaos. When he started talking about his only friend, I wondered how I could be so close to him and not know who this friend was. A friend who listened to all his thoughts and feelings, silently calming him.

As he described his friend Alex, I realized he was talking about his diary. His description was so vivid and metaphorical that it left me shocked and confused. It seemed like he was sad and searching for someone to heal him and listen to him. But when he couldn't find anyone to help, he turned to his diary and wrote his first entry.

Adam had felt the tremendous pain and sorrow of living. He was searching for someone to take away his burdens, and I wasn't able to help him. It was haunting to realize that those years were some of the most painful of his life. He was stuck in the intense and deep depths of life, watching everything around him.

"Searching for Purpose.
A hope to stay alive.
Something to Live for."

I remembered the things Adam had told me once. Something had happened in his life, and he had lost all hope. That period was the most difficult phase of his life. I felt if he had someone to take care of his emotions and health back then, we might still see the cheerful and happy Adam I had known since childhood, not the cold person I saw now.

"Oh, fuck!" I exclaimed.

Adam, with his deadly dangerous eyes, watched me exclaiming and looked into my eyes. I was sweating profusely, water flooding like a monsoon outbreak.

"Adam, listen, what happened is..."

"Hey boy! Just drop it, man. Don't look at that book again," Adam said.

"Sure, brother!" I replied.

"Yeah! Fine then. It kinda pisses me off when someone looks into my private stuff," Adam said in his most silent tone, his eyes cold.

The situation got sorted out, but it felt like being caught in a crossfire or doing espionage in a foreign country. These two scenarios were the easiest way to describe what had just happened. He was angry, but I knew him; he just tried to control his anger with utmost importance. He believed that anger made a person weak. Decisions made in anger could be the deadliest and worst decisions of your life, leading you to despair.

But Adam had already gained control over his anger. I remembered once when he had gone through a sad, ghosting phase. He was so pissed off and frustrated. That was the first time I saw him in his most intense angry mode.

"Look, Adam," I said, trying to break the tension, "I didn't mean to invade your privacy. I was just curious. We've always been open with each other."

"I get that," Adam replied, his tone softer now. "But some things are personal. That book... it's my way of dealing with stuff."

"I understand," I said, feeling a bit relieved. "I just wish I could have been there for you when you needed someone."

"You are here now," he said, a hint of a smile appearing on his face. "And that's what matters."

We stood there for a moment, the tension slowly dissipating. I realized how much he had been through and how he had managed to come out stronger. The bond between us felt renewed, stronger than before.

I remembered the day when Adam's anger boiled over. He was just like:

"You know, that fucking bitch sucks!" he ranted. "That motherfucking whore, how can she just talk all good and suddenly start fucking around?"

"This thing pisses me off, bro! You see, you see?"

"That son of a bitch, some random shit-obsessed fuck!"

"She ain't getting off my nerves. I should never have approached her in good faith."

"This sucks, bro! Ah...h...h..."

"Why ain't she getting off my mind..."

"Fuck her, fuck you! You bitch... Damn motherfucking whore!... Ah...h...h..."

That day, I understood how sensitive he was back then. Now, he's a man with a poker face, and no one can figure out what's going on in his mind. Shitty-shitty talks and a cold-blooded demeanor—these are the two faces of the same person standing in front of me.

"Adam," I said, remembering that time. "You were so different back then."

He looked at me, his eyes unreadable. "People change," he replied, his voice steady.

"Do you ever think about that time?" I asked. "About how angry you were, how much pain you were in?"

He paused, seeming to consider his words carefully. "Yeah, sometimes," he admitted. "But it's like looking at a different person. I've learned to control it, to channel it."

"I wish I could have helped you more back then," I said, feeling a pang of guilt.

"You did what you could," he said, his tone softening. "We were all just trying to figure things out. I've moved on, and I've learned to deal with things in my own way."

We stood there in silence for a moment, the weight of the past hanging between us. It was clear that those years had left a deep impact on him, shaping him into the man he was today—calm on the outside, but with a storm that had once raged within.

"You're stronger now," I said finally. "But if you ever need to talk, I'm here."

"Thanks," he said, a hint of a smile on his lips. "That means a lot."

And with that, we moved forward, leaving the ghosts of the past where they belonged—behind us, but never forgotten.

"Okay! Come downstairs if you're done wandering around my room," Adam called.

"Yeah, wait a minute," I replied.

I got up and put the book back in its place. Adam didn't seem to take any precautions to hide it or keep it with himself. I didn't bother him about it again. My mind was occupied with analyzing Adam's mood. I followed him downstairs. He had brewed some coffee for us. I sat by the dining area, which was beautifully decorated with items imported from Europe. The elegance and aristocratic vibes were everywhere, soothing and nice. I observed Adam as he poured the brewed coffee into cups. The cups were pieces of art—elegant and beautiful. I couldn't take my eyes off anything. The beauty and elegance were overwhelming. I knew Adam was passionate about art and culture, but seeing everything here with such fine beauty was extraordinary.

He brought the coffee cups and sat in front of me.

"Have some," he said.

"Sure," I replied.

"So, what was it that you were looking for in my room?" he asked.

"Nothing, I was just exploring and suddenly found that book," I said.

"And?" he prompted.

"I just took a peek, nothing more," I assured him.

"Okay! I trust you then," he said.

I could sense a lingering tension, so I decided to steer the conversation to safer ground. "Your place is really beautiful, Adam. The way you've decorated it is incredible."

"Thanks," he said, his tone softening. "I've put a lot of effort into it. Art and culture are my passions, as you know."

"It really shows," I said. "Every piece here feels like it has a story."

"That's the idea," he said, smiling. "I wanted a place that reflects who I am and what I love."

We sipped our coffee in silence for a moment, appreciating the ambiance.

He nodded, a thoughtful expression on his face. "You know, it's nice to have a friend like you who understands."

"Likewise, Adam," I said, feeling a warm sense of camaraderie.

After a while, he looked at the clock. "I think you should leave; it's already getting quite late."

"Sure," I said, finishing my coffee. We completed our little chit-chat, and I got up to leave.

Adam was assisting me to the exit. When it was time to say the final goodbye, I asked him one last question.

"Do you still live alone?"

"Does it bother you?" he replied.

I was taken aback. I had asked a question and, in turn, got asked another one. Typical of him. Then he told me to wait for a few minutes and went upstairs. I wondered what he was up to. Did he think I had robbed him of his secrets or something more?

He returned with a khaki-colored envelope, which had a little something inside.

"You might find the answer in here," he said with a smile, waving his hand before closing the door.

I was curious about what was inside the envelope, but I decided to respect him and open it once I got home. I got into my car, started the engine, pressed the pedals, and accelerated towards home.

The night was beautiful, with fog hanging around everywhere. The streets grew darker as I took some local roads. Despite the darkness, the weather was stunning. Seeing the stars in the dark sky after so many years felt amazing. It was a feeling I couldn't shake off my head. So peaceful, it felt like heaven had landed here.

As I drove, I thought about how this beautiful world couldn't stay forever. The romance of life doesn't last long for most people. Only a few lucky ones experience lasting romance. I wasn't one of them, but the feeling this night gave me was similar to those rare moments of pure bliss.

> *"Every season brings with it something,*
> *Something to look for,*
> *Something to enjoy for,*
> *Something to cheer for,*
> *Something to live for,*
> *But that something doesnt stay forever,*
> *And soon welcomes the reality of mischief,*
> *I dont know how I can be one for something,*
> *But the flow of time takes everything with it*
> *"*

Singing songs and crafting poems in this beautiful weather is what gives humanity the purpose of living in art. Appreciating the beauty of this world is what we should strive for. Rather than succumbing to jealousy, we should live in appreciation of the beautiful things around us—be it a person, a prose, a poem, or a piece of art.

Soon, the dark road ended, and I found myself on a highway. The serene beauty of nature vanished, replaced by the chaos of traffic and the light pollution of the night. I accelerated my car and, within half an hour, arrived home.

I got out of the car, grabbed the package from the passenger seat, closed the door, and locked the car. As I walked towards my door, I realized something—the envelope had taken the shape of its contents. The feeling was familiar, like something I had touched before, perhaps a book I had read. But I didn't know for sure what was inside. I hurriedly walked towards my house, unlocked the door, hung my coat on the hanger, and removed my shoes.

I moved towards the sofa in the living room and jumped onto it like I was competing in an athletic event. It felt wonderful, like jumping on something that wouldn't hurt. In life, we jump for many things, and most of them hurt. We jump for the best seat in a movie theater, we jump for the best possible college, then for the best job. But these jumps often come with pain. The most perilous jump of all is proposing to someone you like. Getting rejected by a college or a job hurts, but you can always try again. When you jump to confess your feelings to someone, rejection can lead to a unique kind of pain and mental turmoil. It's a hurt that lingers, making you question who you are and what you've achieved. It feels like all your accomplishments become meaningless.

I sat up properly and took the envelope, tearing it open as if it were a package. Inside was something that took me by surprise. It was the very thing I had been searching for, the thing I had peeked at earlier. I couldn't believe my eyes—Adam had given me the same diary he had written and that I had briefly read.

The note read:

> *"Dear friend,*
> *This key opens the doors to where you'll find my thoughts and feelings. Perhaps this will answer your question and give you a glimpse of something.*
> *Adam"*

I felt a surge of emotions as I read the note. Adam had opened up a part of his life to me that he kept hidden from the world. I decided to visit him again soon, hoping to understand him better and be there for him as a true friend.

The doorbell rang all of a sudden. Who could be here at this hour? I moved slowly towards the door, frightened, holding a stick in one hand just in case someone tried to break in. (Sometimes I wonder if "burglary" is associated with Bulgaria, the southeastern European country). The bell rang again, this time accompanied by a fierce knock. I looked out but couldn't see anything through the fog that had settled over the neighborhood. My only choice was to open the door.

Slowly, I cracked the door open and peeked out. To my surprise...

"It's you!"

"Long time, no see."

"Ha-ha! But why didn't you open the door sooner?"

"Oh! Sorry, sorry..."

"It's fine. Just open it."

"Sure."

The large wooden door, swaying like a prize in a tug-of-war between friends, finally gave way. A blast of cold, sizzling wind rushed in, sending a shiver down my spine.

"Uuuu!" I exclaimed. "It's so cold outside. Come in, quickly."

"Yeah, yeah."

She removed her coat, a piece I hadn't seen before. It was a real work of art, with soft, fluffy fur combined with intricate leatherwork. Simply beautiful.

"When did you get that?" I asked.

"Ah! I just bought it on my trip to see the Northern Lights."

"Northern Lights? Seriously?"

"Yup, bro!"

"They must be amazing. The perfect combination of the beauty of space and nature."

"They are. It's like watching a live painting in the sky. The colors, the movement, it's all so surreal. You should definitely go see them sometime."

"I would love to. Maybe one day. So, how was the trip overall?"

"It was incredible. The cold was intense, but it was worth it. I met some wonderful people, and the experience was beyond words."

"Sounds like a dream. I've always wanted to see the Northern Lights. Did you take any pictures?"

"I did, but honestly, pictures don't do it justice. You have to see it with your own eyes to really understand."

We chatted more about her trip, the places she visited, the food she tried, and the stories she gathered along the way.

"Ah! Let's end it here," she said finally.

"Seems like you're tired," I noted.

"Yes, it was a long journey."

"Have some water, and let's get some sleep."

"That would be the best."

I fetched a glass of water for her. She drank it gratefully and then we headed upstairs to her room. As she settled in, I couldn't help but think about the beautiful stories she might have brought with her. It was a reminder of the wonders of the world, even on a cold, foggy night like this.

With that, we ended our conversation and decided to go to our beds. The diary was still there in the living room. I thought for a minute—should I hide it somewhere or just leave it as it is? I decided to leave it where it was and went to sleep.

It had been five years since Marie and I started living together, but we never shared the same room. We believed that even if we loved each other, there should be some amount of personal space. Each of us needed a place to reflect on our true selves, a space filled with our own emotions and nature. This notion of having our own space made us appreciate the importance of having someone in our lives.

Feeling tired and drowsy, I moved towards my bed. As soon as I reached the corner, I fell onto it, exhausted.

TWO
THE FORGOTTEN PAST

"He was scammed by his girlfriend after five long years of relationship..."

"Hey, good morning! What are you doing?" I asked.

"Nothing! But I think I found something interesting," Marie sounded somewhat suspicious.

"What's so interesting this morning?" I asked, moving towards her excitedly.

But when I got a glimpse of the book—the diary—I felt a spark of tremendous anger and nervousness surge through my body. I felt the need to snatch the book and retreat to my room. It was a violation of the privacy we had always respected between each other. She had picked up something that was not hers, not even mine, but Adam's. Something so personal. I shouldn't have left it on the table last night.

"Did you use to have a girlfriend in the past?" she angrily scolded.

"It doesn't matter anymore. What matters is you touching and looking into someone's personal stuff."

"This thing, okay. But it's not yours, I guess."

"Hmmmm..."

"What, you don't have any answers? But this thing has some stuff about you in here."

"Really?"

"Wait, just give that back to me."

"No, not at all. I might disclose some more stuff about you."

"You liar!"

"Wait!"

With that, she took the book and ran towards her room hurriedly while I tried to chase her down the hall. But then I smelled something bad, something was off in the house, something was burning. Instead of chasing her, I returned to the kitchen and found that the food I had left on the stove had turned completely black, emitting a toxic smell of ash and carbon throughout the house. I quickly turned off the burner, poured water over the charred remains, opened all the windows for ventilation, and sat on the sofa, thinking about what all things Adam might have written about me in the diary.

I started recalling the period covered in the diary, trying to piece together my life at that point. As I reflected, Marie's question echoed in my mind: "Did you have a girlfriend in the past?" The year 2014 stood out. I struggled to remember any specific girl I was romantically involved with that year. Back then, I was a cold student, not much into romantic pursuits. But as I delved deeper into my memories, they began to resurface, making me laugh at how charismatic those times were. Childhood was so much fun and carefree unless you chose to take on stress.

Suddenly, it hit me: 2014 was the year I had my first breakup with a girl named Isabella. I had been with her for a long time. Our relationship began when I was just 15 and lasted over four years. I was truly in love with her. But falling in love with her had its consequences. It isolated me from the boys in my class, and slowly, even the people closest to me abandoned me.

This is the story I needed to share, especially with Marie, to settle everything down peacefully. Sonia had brought chaos into my life back then, and even today, her name and the memories still stirred chaos. I didn't know where she was or what she was doing now, but sometimes I thought about her because she was my first love. I had loved her deeply, but nature decides what you get to keep. The things you cherish most often aren't yours in your early days. Everything fades eventually. I don't know what kind of chain reactions and other forces cause things to vanish, but nothing is permanent, and everything is temporary.

Those were mischievous days. I had been newly admitted to a new school in a new city. This town was different from others, as I felt at first glance. Due to my father's profession, we moved from town to town, city to city. When I found out we had to leave my previous school, I cried and resisted the move. I didn't know if it was because of my bond with this other girl *Amelia* or because I had spent a long time in that city, enjoying every place. I roamed and played here and there, moving through the trees, playing on the ground, laughing, crying, enjoying every moment of that peaceful life.

> **"How happy I was when I was young**
> **Laughing, crying, singing with passing time**
> **How happy all started having"**

Those were the happiest days of my life, filled with playful and joyous moments with Amelia. I still remember the time I lost my lunchbox on the way to school. I was crying a lot because of my empty stomach and the fear of being scolded at home for losing something personal. She sat beside me, saw my tears, and wiped them away with her napkin. It was such a kind gesture, and then she offered me her food. We sat on the same bench, sharing her lunchbox, and eating together. That was the first time I had a crush on someone, and it was her. From that day onwards, we shared everything between us. Our lives became intertwined with every passing moment. Our classmates often teased us, calling us Romeo and Juliet or Adam and Eve. Some were jealous, while others enjoyed seeing the stories they had read come to life. Initially, the teasing made me want to cry, but she reassured me.

"Why feel sorry?" she said. "There's nothing wrong with what we're doing. We're friends who enjoy each other's company. Can't we be friends with someone of a different gender?"

Her words were mature beyond her age, and her perspective comforted me. We started ignoring the teasing, and eventually, it stopped. The classroom felt calm and peaceful. These memories are precious to me.

One day, during the winter, the sun shone brighter than usual. My sweaters felt too warm, so I decided to take mine off. As I tried to remove it, the sweater got stuck around my neck. I struggled, feeling embarrassed as some boys laughed and slapped me on the back. I called for help, but they continued to mock me. They said this wouldn't have happened if my Juliet had been there. She was sick that day, and I felt her absence keenly. The classroom bell rang, and our teacher walked in.

"What are you doing, boy?" the teacher asked.

"Nothing, ma'am. I'm stuck while trying to remove my sweater," I replied, my hands partially caught in the sweater.

"Come here, I'll help you," she said.

I moved blindly through the classroom, bumping into tables and chairs, much to the amusement of my classmates. Finally, the teacher helped me remove the sweater. I felt relieved but also captivated by the pleasant scent of her perfume. After settling down, the teacher made an announcement.

"From next week onwards your holidays are going to start, so for this year the school has organised a 3-day trip to an island in Pacific Ocean"

"From next week onwards, your holidays will begin. The school has organized a three-day trip to an island in the Pacific Ocean."

"Wowwwww!" everyone shouted.

"Silence! You need to register with the set amount and bring a parental consent form by Friday. No new entries will be allowed after that," she continued.

I felt a wave of nervousness and a mix of emotions flooding into my head. I was both happy and sad. Happy at the thought of going on a trip to the Pacific, but sad because she might not be able to come. The idea of going alone filled me with dread. As our teacher explained the details of the trip, I found myself praying she would recover in time to join us. I decided to visit her home that day, armed with all the information about the trip, and do everything I could to help her get well quickly. I even planned to convince her parents to let her go, promising to take responsibility for her.

Big words for a little boy, perhaps, but that's how childhood ambition works. Looking back, I realize that childhood is the best phase of our lives. Everything seems to go smoothly; we don't have to worry about much because our needs are taken care of. Our expectations from life are minimal, but our ambitions and curiosity are at their peak. As we grow older, we sadly lose that simplicity and wonder.

> *"How good it was when I was young*
> *Nothing to care for long enough*
> *Delve into passion and curiosity for fun*
> *But slowly everything is going to degrade*
> *Long enough before anything happens*
> *Soon welcomed us to the cursed adult world*
> *Now I want to wake up and strive for the one*
> *I was living back when I was young"*

The final bell of school rang, and I hurriedly packed my bag, eager to start my mission. As I stepped outside, the cold wind hit me, making me regret removing my sweater earlier. The temperature had dropped, and I shivered as I walked to the nearby convenience store. My resolve wavered for a moment, but I quickly pushed on, determined to help her get better.

At the store, I looked for a charm that might help her recover from her cold. I found one and paid for it with my monthly pocket money, money I usually spent on chocolates and toffees. But if I couldn't sacrifice my sweets for her, what kind of man would I be when I grew up? With the charm in hand, I headed toward her house.

The path to her house was in the opposite direction of mine, and as the sun began to set, the cold intensified. I took a public transport bus, something I had done alone since I was young. It felt like another task I needed to complete on my journey toward maturity. I was becoming more self-reliant, and this determination fueled me.

I took a public transport bus to get to my destination. I had been using this bus alone since I was young, having to manage most things by myself. This journey felt like another task I needed to complete to survive. Gradually, I was becoming more mature. Someday, I thought, I would be a responsible citizen of this country. This determination ignited a fire within me, filling me with motivation.

After a ten-minute bus ride, I arrived at my stop. The terrain near her place was uneven, situated on the slope of a hill. I remembered the way and the landmarks she had pointed out when I once came here with her. Her parents were so kind to me, offering every piece of the delicious food they had brought back from their vacation in Europe that spring. Her house was as big as a mansion, sprawling over a large area and complete with a swimming pool. That might be the reason why she excelled in swimming competitions.

As I walked through the neighborhood, I admired the large, elegant houses. Each one seemed to tell a story of its own.

As I walked through the neighborhood, an old lady called out to me.

"Hey, young boy, come here!"

I was frightened at first, thinking she might be a kidnapper or something sinister. Growing up, we were always warned about strangers: don't take anything from them, don't trust them, and so on. But as I looked at the old woman more closely, I realized she was calling me because she needed help with the package and bag she was carrying.

I walked toward her and asked, "What happened?"

"Uhh! Hey, could you please help me take this bag to the nearby nursing home? It's just around that corner."

"Nursing home? What does that mean?" I asked, puzzled.

"It's a kind of day-boarding school for old people," she explained curtly.

She didn't bother to clarify further, and I took her words at face value. Reflecting on it now, I realize how self-centered we become as we grow older. In our youth, we chase materialistic goals—fun, enjoyment, spouse, children, money, a house—and neglect the ones who raised us, the ones who contributed so much to our lives. Our parents, who were once our entire world, become secondary to our pursuits.

I took the bag she handed me and walked with her to the nearby nursing home. When we arrived, she gave me 50 bucks and thanked me, her eyes welling up as she spoke.

"Remember to stay kind as you grow older, especially to your parents," she said, tears now streaming down her cheeks.

"I'm sorry, please don't cry, Grandma," I said, feeling helpless.

"Oh!" She started rubbing her eyes and walked towards the entrance of the nursing home, waving goodbye to me.

Watching her go, I felt a deep sense of sadness and resolve. I promised myself I would never forget this encounter and the lesson it taught me about kindness and the importance of family.

I looked at my watch; I was running late. I thought about my mom, who was probably worried about why I hadn't come back from school yet. I decided to hurry towards her house and call my mom from there to let her know I was checking on my friend.

After walking for 10-15 minutes through the narrow roads of the neighborhood, I reached a main road. Around the corner was her house. I knocked on the gate, and to my surprise, it triggered a bell inside the house. This must be some kind of new technology, I thought, because I didn't see any visible bell.

Her mom came out, wondering who was there. I was still short at that time, so she didn't see me immediately.

"It's me, Aunty!" I shouted.

"Oh! So it's you. Come, come inside," she said warmly.

The gate opened automatically, and I walked towards the house alongside her mom.

"Sit, child. I will call her," she said.

"Sure, Aunty," I replied.

As her mother went upstairs to call her, my curiosity kicked in. I started looking around, hoping to find something interesting. The last time I visited, I found a new game that hadn't even been launched in the country yet—probably something she had brought back from Europe. This time, my eyes fell on a painting.

It was unusual and difficult to understand, perhaps the work of a famous artist. The painting was so large it covered an entire wall. The colors were deep, and the texture and brushstrokes were wonderfully intricate. Artists, I thought, are those who follow their passion no matter the hardships they face. They are so obsessed and skilled at what they do that their ultimate success brings a sense of fulfillment to their lives.

Lost in admiration of the painting, I barely noticed when her mom and my friend came back downstairs.

Soon, after a few minutes, I heard a voice.

"Huh huh!" She coughed.

"Oh! Hey, are you okay?" I asked, concerned.

"Yeah, I'm fine, but these past few days have been tough," she replied.

"Yeah, it must be difficult," I sympathized.

"But Mom was here to look after me," she added.

Thinking about her mention of her mom, I glanced at the clock on the wall. It was getting late, and I hadn't informed my own mother that I was here checking on my friend.

"Yeah, Aunty must have taken good care of you. She sure is a good mother," I said.

"So, how are you doing?" she asked.

"Good. I just came by to check on you since you haven't been around for the past few days," I said. "Hey, look, this is what I got for you. I bought this get-well-soon charm."

"Ahh, that's so sweet of you. Now, I think I'll get well soon, especially since you brought this," she said, smiling.

"I hope the same from my heart," I murmured.

"Did you say something?" she asked.

"Nothing, I was just thinking that you should get well soon," I said.

"And one more thing—" I started to say, but we were interrupted by her mother's voice and the sound of footsteps approaching. Her mom came in carrying snacks and tea for both of us.

"Hey, children, first eat something," she said.

"Yummy! Now that I'm feeling better than yesterday, I don't have to eat that bland soup," my friend said.

"Amelia, no talking like that, bad girl," her mom chided gently.

"Sorry, Mom!"

"Hey, boy, have some snacks," her mom offered.

"Yeah, sure, Aunty!" I replied.

"So, what were you two discussing?" her mom asked.

"Mom, look, he bought a get-well-soon charm just for me so that I can get better soon," Amelia said.

"Oh, young boy, already taking care of a girl," her mom teased.

I started blushing at the words of praise and affirmation from both of them, feeling nervous and uncomfortable. I looked around, trying to hide my embarrassment.

"You're looking red. Are you alright?" Amelia asked, noticing my flushed face.

"Hmm!" her mom laughed, watching us together.

"It looks like you two should play, and I'll be in the kitchen," her mom said, leaving us alone.

They were quite wealthy but yet they didnt had an chef in their house. Seemed like they were rooted to some of the traditional values or they might have preferred having cook by themselves or else chef might be on holiday.

"Hey, so what should we play?" she asked.

"I think we can play cards," I suggested.

We both got up from the sofa and started moving toward the stairs, as her room was upstairs. She was wearing a shark suit that looked kind of funny. As she walked in front of me, the tail of her suit swirled from left to right, and it made me chuckle. I was determined to play a little prank by stepping on her tail. It was a childish thing to do, something I might not have done if I were older.

I put my foot on her tail, and her movements came to a sudden halt. She bumped into me and we both fell to the ground, with her landing on top of me. I was the one who had intended to have fun at her expense, but instead, I was the one who ended up getting hurt. A sudden "ouch" escaped my lips, but I was ready to take responsibility for my mischief.

As we lay there, a different atmosphere filled the air—something almost romantic. We looked at each other, smiled, and then burst out laughing. It was a cute and peaceful moment, but soon reality intruded, reminding us that we were just two young children who weren't supposed to be doing this kind of thing.

We got up, and I apologized for being mischievous. Then I started running upstairs, with her following close behind. We entered her room, and she told me to sit on the bed while she searched for the card deck. She rummaged through a drawer, found the cards, and then sat beside me.

"Which game do you want to play?" she asked.

More than the game, I was captivated by the aura surrounding me. I was dreaming, nervous, and feeling uncomfortable but in a good way. What it was, I didn't know; how it was, I didn't know; when it might happen, I didn't know. But the feeling of experiencing such emotions in those brief moments fulfilled my life in a way I couldn't describe.

"Hey, are you listening?" she waved her hand in front of my face.

"Uhhh! Hh, yeah, absolutely. I'm listening."

"So, which game?"

I suddenly remembered that I had been out for quite a while and hadn't informed my mom about my whereabouts. I decided that I needed to leave as she might be worried about me.

"Ha, I think I should leave. It's already late."

"Oh! But we didn't even start playing."

"Yeah, but you know, I didn't tell my mom I'd be late. She might be worried."

"Okay..."

"Oh, I almost forgot to tell you!"

"What?"

"The main reason I came here was because of the school trip that's organized for next week."

I started explaining to her everything that had happened at school. I told her about the details of the trip and how much fun it would be. I tried my best to convince her to come along, emphasizing how great it would be if she joined me.

"I really think you should come. It won't be the same without you."

She looked thoughtful, then sighed. "I'll have to think about it. I'm not sure if I can."

She called her mom, and when her mom came to the room, she asked what was going on. Amelia explained about the trip and how she wanted to go with me.

"Mom, I really want to go on this trip with him. It sounds like so much fun, and I think it would be good for me."

Her mom looked concerned. "But your health hasn't been great lately, dear. We need to make sure you're fully recovered."

"I know, Mom. But if I'm healthy by then, can I please go? You can talk to the school and register me for the trip."

Her mom hesitated, then nodded. "If you get better before the trip, I'll talk to the school and register you. But you need to get all your work done and make sure you're well enough to go."

"Thank you, Mom!"

I stood up. "Aunty, I need to leave now. You can continue with your work."

"Hey, listen up! I'll drop you off."

"Sure, Aunty."

Her mom went downstairs to pack up everything and clean the kitchen. While she was busy, Amelia came from behind and hugged me. I felt a sensation of warmth; it was so peaceful and nice. The feeling of two hearts pumping together simultaneously, filled with the combination of two different auras, the sound of breaths quietly running into each other's ears—it was like a comet approaching or me moving through different dimensions of the world at the same time. That day turned out to be one of the best in the world. So nice, uhhh. Why can't this moment stay forever?

Amelia pulled back and smiled. "Thank you for coming today. It really means a lot."

I smiled back. "Of course. I just want you to get better and join us on the trip. It wouldn't be the same without you."

She nodded. "I'll do my best. And I'll make sure to take care of myself so I can go."

Her mom called out from downstairs, "Alright, let's go. I'm ready."

"You ready, boy?" Amelia's mom called out.

"Sure, I'm coming," I replied.

"You," she addressed Amelia, "stay and rest quietly at home. When you've finished everything, you can go."

I gently removed Amelia's hands from around me and waved goodbye. I then headed downstairs and joined her mom. She led the way to the garage, which was as beautiful as the rest of their house. Inside were two cars: an SUV and a sleek sedan, a BMW 7-Series.

Her mom took out the BMW sedan, a car that exuded luxury with its sleek design and advanced features. The exterior was a glossy black, reflecting the light like a polished gem. The interior was equally impressive, with leather seats that were both comfortable and elegant. The dashboard featured a state-of-the-art infotainment system, and the ride was smooth and quiet, a testament to the engineering prowess behind it.

As we drove, her mom asked, "So, what's this school trip all about?"

"It's a week-long trip to the Pacific coast," I explained. "We'll be exploring different places, learning about marine life, and even doing some camping. I really hope Amelia can join us. It won't be the same without her."

Her mom smiled. "That sounds wonderful. I'm sure she'd love to go, and it would be good for her too. She just needs to recover fully first."

We soon arrived at my house. I got out of the car and headed to the front door, eager to tell my mom about my day. I rang the bell, but there was no response. It seemed like no one was home. I then tried knocking on the door, but to my surprise, it was open.

Her mom came up behind me after parking the car on the street. "What happened?" she asked.

"No one is responding, and the door is open. I think we should go inside."

"Sure," she agreed.

As I stepped inside, I looked around, calling out for my mom. I ran through the corridors, searching for any signs of her or any indication that someone might have broken in. But the house was empty. I asked Amelia's mom to try calling my mom.

I found our phonebook in a drawer and gave her my mom's number. She dialed it on her phone. The first ring went unanswered, as did the second. Finally, on the third ring, my mom picked up. Her voice was fraught with worry and tension.

"Hello! Is this Miss...?"

"Yes, who is this speaking?"

"Uh, I'm the mom of your son's friend. He came by our place to visit my daughter, who was sick."

"Oh, really! Where is he now?"

"We're both at your house."

"Okay! Thank God! Please wait with him. I was at the school, checking if he was still there because he hadn't come home at his usual time."

With that, my mom hung up, and we both waited for her to come back.

As we waited, Amelia's mom tried to make small talk to ease my worry. "So, what else do you like to do besides visiting sick friends and going on school trips?"

I smiled, appreciating her effort. "I like reading and playing soccer. And sometimes, I just like to explore new places around the neighborhood."

She nodded. "That's good. It's important to have hobbies and interests. They help you grow and learn new things."

I nodded, feeling a bit more relaxed. We continued chatting until my mom arrived, her face a mixture of relief and concern.

"Oh, thank goodness!" she exclaimed as she hugged me. "I was so worried!"

"I'm sorry, Mom," I said. "I should have told you where I was going."

"It's okay, just make sure to let me know next time," she said, then turned to Amelia's mom.

"Thank you so much for bringing him home."

"It was no problem at all," she replied with a warm smile. "I'm glad we could help."

After thanking her once more, my mom and I watched as she got back into her BMW and drove away. I felt a sense of relief and gratitude, knowing I was home safe and had wonderful friends who cared about me.

That was a vivid memory from my childhood, but the girl wasn't Sonia, and Amelia wasn't my girlfriend. She was just a good friend. Remembering this old memory brought a smile to my face and a sense of calmness. Those days were truly some of the most beautiful days of my life.

Suddenly, I remembered that I needed to sort things out with Marie. I hurriedly ran to Marie's room and asked her to open the door. She wasn't responding. I apologized and promised her that I would tell her everything she needed to know. After a moment, she accepted my request and opened the door.

When I saw her, her face was red, and tears were streaming down her cheeks. I felt a pang of guilt and sadness. I gently wiped away her tears and hugged her. I didn't know what had happened to put her in such a devastating state. I led her to the sofa, and we sat beside each other. I took a deep breath and began explaining everything.

I started with the story of Sonia.

"It was the first day of my new school," I began. "I was a shy little kid, wandering aimlessly in the corridors. One day, we had a reshuffling of our seating positions in class, and I was allotted a new seat beside a girl named Sonia. She was a bright student, one of the top scorers, but she had some health issues. From that day until the next reshuffling, Sonia and I became close friends."

Marie listened intently, her tears subsiding as I continued.

"Sonia and I would talk, joke, and laugh together. We shared secrets and supported each other. Life started to feel exciting again, and I looked forward to each school day. I dreaded the end of the school day and eagerly awaited the next morning when I could see her again."

I paused, recalling the fond memories of those days.

"One day, I got overwhelmed by my feelings for her. I couldn't keep them bottled up any longer. I decided to express how I felt and proposed to her, hoping to take our friendship to another level."

Marie looked at me with a mixture of curiosity and concern.

"How did she respond?" she asked softly.

"She was surprised," I said, smiling at the memory.

"She didn't expect it at all. Sonia told me she valued our friendship deeply and didn't want anything to change that. She was kind and gentle in her response, and though I was disappointed, I understood."

But after a month or so, things started to take a different turn. Sonia knew I had feelings for her, but we weren't talking as much or spending time together like we used to. This started to make her feel neglected and left out. She began experiencing a whole set of different emotions and started taking more days off from school. Watching this, I decided one day to visit her home and see why she was taking more days off than ever before.

When I arrived at her house, no one was there. Sonia opened the door for me and invited me inside. As I went inside and sat on the sofa, she offered me some tea and snacks and asked if we should sit in her room. We both went to her room, with her holding a tray of tea and biscuits. We sat on the floor of her room, which was filled with cute little toys. I looked around, taking in everything, while she asked me to have the tea and biscuits.

As we ate, I started our conversation, gently leading it to why she wasn't coming to school regularly and what had happened. Her expression changed drastically; she was blushing, her face turning a deep red. She hesitated, but I kept asking why she wouldn't come to school, if something was wrong, or if anything had happened. Finally, she couldn't control her emotions and feelings anymore and burst out.

"It was because you weren't talking to me the way you used to and making me feel special like before," she said, her voice trembling. "And also, one more thing..." She paused, taking a deep breath, and then the three magical words finally came out of her mouth: "I LOVE YOU!"

I was shocked and stunned, thinking about how she had turned me down before and wondering how this could happen. While I was lost in my thoughts, she moved toward me, grabbed me, and kissed me. The kiss was so passionate. The house was empty, and a bizarre silence filled the room. We both soaked in the heat of the moment, enjoying each other. Her lips were soft and warm, and the kiss felt like an eternity. Our hearts beat in sync, and everything else seemed to fade away. The room felt alive with a mixture of newfound love and lingering uncertainty.

Marie interrupted my recollection. "Okay, okay, let it be. Tell me, skipping this part, how did both of you end things?"

"I think that's something you already read in the diary," I said, trying to avoid the painful memory. "Please, I don't want to talk about it. It's a bitter memory. I've told you a lot already, and now I don't feel there's any point in telling you more because now we both are together and the past doesn't matter anymore."

Marie looked calm and seemed to be relaxing a bit. "Okay, okay! I get it now," she said softly.

"Alright then! Can I get the book back?" I asked, reaching out.

"Here it is," she said, handing it to me. Then she hesitated before adding, "But can we both read it together?"

I paused, thinking for a moment. Should we read it together? After a minute, I realized that Marie and I were now a part of each other's lives. There were no more secrets to hide.

"Sure, we can read it together," I said, smiling. "We're one and the same now. It shouldn't matter if we both read it."

Marie's face lit up with a smile. "Thank you," she said, looking relieved. "I just want to understand everything, and I think sharing this will help."

We settled down on the sofa, the diary open between us.

THREE
EARLY DAYS

As Marie and I turned the pages of Adam's diary, the entries drew me into deep, wondrous thoughts. Each word felt like a portal to the past that Adam had hidden from us.

"*December 17, 2014*

Dear Friend,

It has been a long time since I last wrote to you. Today, I feel compelled to discuss what I believe is the most pressing matter: our future prospects. Lately, I have been haunted by a profound emptiness in my heart. This past year has been a whirlwind of ups and downs, and my mind is entangled in endless thoughts.

I find myself questioning the one thing I truly seek in life. Is it the composure that comes with success, or is it the deep yearning to fill the void left in my heart with someone I can trust and love as I do my mother? This pervasive feeling of loneliness in a highly competitive and rapidly developing environment gnaws at my soul. I long to eradicate this isolation, which plagues me in this foreign land, far from the comfort of home—a place that would soon become my new abode.

Home fills me with joy, and my family transforms my loneliness into happiness. Yet here, I struggle to find that special someone. Someone to whom I can reveal my true self,

someone to cry for,
someone to cry on,
someone to care for,
someone to show kindness.

I desire someone to trust and to make this world a place with better meaning and fulfillment for me. Nevertheless, the fear of losing someone I love paralyzes me, making me abstain from the pain and suffering that love inevitably brings.

I resolve to achieve a state of cold, emotionless composure, a poker face that reveals nothing. No reaction, no feelings—only a shield against the pain and sadness that love entails. Loving someone brings joy, but it also brings the inevitable balance of cheerfulness and sorrow. My mind desperately seeks a way to eradicate this immense, continuous sadness. I have not felt the thrill and joy of life for a long time. I yearn for it, but not at the cost of future pain.

Life feels like a living hell without a kindred spirit to transform it temporarily into heaven. Yet, when that soul fades, reality returns with immense pain. There seems to be no purpose in living a life devoid of hope and goals. We have become mere task performers, executing daily routines year after year just to sustain our existence. Dreams and imagination die as we confront the harsh reality of a world our loved ones, our parents, shielded us from when we were young.

We are all at the mercy of a higher power, a force that orchestrates this grand game from some distant point in the universe. This power has rendered us incapable of seeing through the grand design. Yet, we are not entirely blind. We grow more knowledgeable and intellectual as we develop, striving to decipher the solutions to the mysteries created by nature or the almighty.

With each passing moment, we become smarter, though only a few of us truly find purpose in life. These few embark on the journey of challenging the almighty, seeking to uncover the deeper meaning of our existence.
Yours,
Adam James
"

"

December 20, 2014
Hey Alex,

Today, I begin the daunting task of writing about the excruciating pain of human existence. The sorrow and anguish of life can feel like the depths of *hell. Life does not always yield favorable outcomes, whether it be in love, joy, fun, or the ambitions thwarted by the pseudo-imposed martial laws stemming from the malevolent auras of people—advisors and colleagues who believe they know what's best for you. Perhaps they are right to some extent, but ultimately, the choices remain in your hands.*

In the 21ˢᵗ century, life has become a farce, embellished by the flashy, voracious tentacles of social media, which only deepen the sense of worthlessness. As young adults, some seize this as an opportunity to devalue others' lives by flaunting false versions of themselves. But at the end of the day, nothing matters more than how utterly broken you feel inside.

Short-term thinking may elevate you to stardom or make you someone others admire, but that becomes meaningless if your inner self remains fractured. Someone must break this cycle of showmanship, insecurity, and the endless pursuit of dopamine-fueled validation. Pause for a moment, sit quietly, and contemplate what you truly desire. What do you genuinely believe is worthy of praise? What is your ultimate goal in life? Will you regret the things you failed to accomplish if you die tomorrow?

Such profound introspection will uncover a myriad of painful, regretful, and joyful experiences that have shaped you. Being solitary may sometimes reward you in your career with glory, money, and extravagance. But if you die alone, with no one to mourn you, it means you have forsaken the essential aspects of a civilized society—those that make life worth living and define our humanity.

Living as an isolated, overly successful individual, devoid of genuine human connection, might grant you luxury, a testament to your hard work and sacrifices. Yet, this path leaves you merciless, and your feelings eroded until you become a mere machine. While it's not inherently wrong to think this way, I know it's not what you always wanted to become. Your past, marked by relentless pain, has shaped your current perspective.

Reflecting on nature, it's as if you were once a living, feeling being, battered by relentless suffering, and chose to become one with mother nature—a non-living piece in the universe's puzzle. Now, free from the endless pain of the living world, you no longer need to worry. You are self-sufficient, evolving like the continents that once formed a single entity but drifted apart over millions of years, becoming uniquely beautiful. Non-living entities endure similarly; over time, the clock of life slows and silences. No longer do you or anyone else worry. Your heart no longer races with love's fervor, the desire extinguished by the overwhelming pain it brings.

Love is a mysterious force, its origin unclear—whether from the heart or brain or perhaps a mere illusion. I never pondered it until I experienced it. Initially, love was profoundly painful. I admired many girls but loved one deeply at a very young age. The constant turmoil of hurt, jealousy, guilt, sorrow, and sadness, coupled with insecurities and poor time management, turned love into a living hell—a sparrow trapped in a golden cage.

This may not be true for everyone, but it shaped who I am today. Every aspect of your present stems from the past, and infinite possibilities arise from each decision, no matter how minute.

I didn't realize it, but now I want to cry and confess everything I feel while writing this. I picture the girl who turned me down because of my own misbehavior. I don't know why I acted that way, perhaps because I was merely interested in her, not in love. I wanted to experience love at 40%, keeping a distance until I determined if my feelings were genuine and compatible and whether this relationship had any future. I didn't want regrets. I wanted to make meaningful contributions to others' lives to be valued. But now, I'm disillusioned by this thing called "LOVE."

I harbor immense anger toward whoever created love, questioning its purpose. I want to love myself, not chase something unattainable and uncertain. This may be the true end, though I remain confused as I pour my heart onto these pages. My heart races, overtaken by wishes, sorrow, and pain. It feels highly unsatisfactory, but this page, my most trustworthy confidant, sees it all.

I am profoundly sad today. It's not just about it; the longing grows deeper, filling my heart and mind. Despite this, I still believe she is attainable, that one day she might be by my side, enduring life's endless ups and downs together. I wanted to cherish her like a diamond. I may end up writing to you again until she forcefully makes me feel ashamed of my feelings. This might not be my last outpouring of love for her.

No... No... No... I've fallen into the infinite loop of my feelings again. I want to be lonely and immensely successful, even at the cost of never experiencing love.
Yours,
Adam James
"

The things I had read just now felt like a deep swirl of emotions floating in Adam's mind. Reading them prompted Marie and me to discuss what was written. Marie was also a bit shocked and deep in thought.

"These writings are quite deep and intense, don't you think?" I asked Marie.

"Absolutely," she replied. "I never thought something like this was brewing inside him."

"It was full of emotions—loneliness, emptiness," I added. "It's heartbreaking to read such a context."

"I don't feel like I have the confidence to read through the rest of this book alone," Marie said, her voice trembling slightly.

"I think you should read it alongside me," I suggested. "We can experience the journey of thought and emotion together."

"You saw that entry dated March 20, 1997?" she asked. "It delves so deeply into the pain of human existence."

"Yes, it was mind-boggling," I agreed.

"Okay, enough for today," Marie said, her voice weary. "I don't think I can handle any more of that right now."

We both stopped reading Adam's diary for the day. I placed it on the table, and we prepared for dinner. It was already late, and the entire day had been a whirlwind of emotions. We had spent hours sharing, recalling, and reading memories from Adam's diary.

As we ate dinner, Marie suddenly asked, "Hey, what do you think about everything we just read and discussed?'

"We've already talked about it," I said, trying to end the conversation. "I don't think we should discuss it any further."

"Come on... I never knew your friend could be like this," she pressed.

I hesitated, unsure if I should share more of Adam's diary with her. "If you're going to judge, maybe you shouldn't read any further."

"No, I won't judge," she assured me. "I was just shocked by what I read."

It seemed she was more interested than ever in reading Adam's diary. Despite everything, I felt a wave of curiosity and excitement that she wouldn't let go of the book now. At the same time, I was still confused, thinking about the ending of that entry. I couldn't connect the dots or understand what Adam meant. He was trying to define love, but for whom? I wasn't getting it. How could I not know anything about it? I tried to recall any small detail, but nothing came to mind. I was lost in my thoughts, trying to link memories, to bring something back from the past. But nothing surfaced. Finally, I told myself that some mysteries need to remain mysteries and should be left as they are.

"Shouldn't we be reading it after dinner?" she asked.

"Sure," I replied.

We continued our conversation as we finished our dinner. Afterward, we washed the dishes and completed our evening chores. I helped Marie with the remaining tasks, and soon enough, our day was done.

The diary lay on the table, waiting for us to return to its pages and uncover more of the past.

FOUR

NO ONE IS WORTH IT!

We both settled into our seats, leaning into each other as we opened the diary. I recalled the last entry I had read and began to read the next iteration.

"*January 4, 2015*
Dear Friend,

Lately, I've been redefining my interests. I find myself drawn to bold and confident women, those who can thrive independently in this world. I believe that someone capable of managing herself is also capable of managing a family effectively. Growing up, both my parents were always busy with work, leaving little time for us to be together. The moments we shared at night were precious, though words fail to capture the depth of my feelings.
Yours,
Adam James"

"January 8, 2015

Dear Alex,

Something I wanted to write out of, "I will forget this feeling someday." Life, it seems, is a horribly dull thing.
Yours,
Adam James"

"January 16, 2015

Dear Alex,

The first time I met her. It was the day of the event, and I was there as an organizer, ensuring the attendees stayed in the auditorium. Two girls, one of whom would soon captivate me, tried to leave. I approached them, urging them to stay. They were insistent on leaving, but I spoke to them about the significance of the event. I told them that even after achieving great things, becoming millionaires, and having everything they could want, they should make God a 10% partner in their success. My passion for the subject eventually convinced them to remain.

I saw her again after the session ended. I was distributing snacks when she approached me. I handed her a packet of snacks. At that moment, she seemed socially awkward—she did not look directly at me, her mouth remained shut, and I did not press her. She took the food silently and quickly left. She was the opposite of the other girl from another town, who was interactive and enjoyed conversing with me. Though I was tempted to flirt, I restrained myself, as my priorities were set differently.

The first girl seemed nice and sweet, silent, and shy like a child—so endearing in her quietness.
Yours,
Adam James"

"**January 21, 2015**
Dear Alex,

Since I first saw you, the race and chase I've been in no longer matter to me. The happiness I was trying to find in material things started to vanish. My life became more lively when I began talking to you. The lost artist within me came back to life. Songs started making sense to me—the music, the lyrics—all began to touch my heart. The melancholy of birdsong felt like the rhythm of life. My mind and soul started finding joy in paintings and poems again. You are the happiness I have been looking for. Please don't send me back into the darkness of sorrow. Light me up with a reason to live.

These past 15 days have been very troublesome for me. Initially, I thought I had lost you when no reply came back. I was in turmoil for a day. Yet still, I long for our meeting. You know, once everything is over, I really hope to have you by my side. I want to meet you, even if it's just once. I want to cherish you.

For the last two years, I have been in some kind of agony. I had lost most things and was in sorrow for a long time. But I think being with you in any form would bring happiness into my life. I want to be happy. I have gone through a lot, and I don't know how much more I can endure.
Yours,

Adam James"

"January 24, 2015
Dear Alex,

Today, I want to share my thoughts on distraction,
hoping to convey my feelings to you.

Here is my rough thought:
I don't know how much I can do for you,
But I don't want to be a distraction.
I want to be someone who cherishes and loves you.
I want to be the catalyst for your growth.

Another thought:
You may take your time—be it days, months, or
even years.
Let the planets change, but my love for you won't
waver.
My feelings for you are immortal, as if blessed by
the gods.
The possibility of having you by my side is better
than the reality of being with anyone else.

Another thought:
I had been living in sorrow,
But now that I have found you,
You have made my eyes shine
And my heart smiles.

And yet another thought:
The right person, the wrong time.
The right script, the wrong line.
The right poem, the wrong rhyme.
And a piece of you that was never mine.
Yours,

Adam James"

"**January 29, 2015**
Dear Alex,

Sometimes, a strange feeling floods through my mind. Will I ever be able to have her? It might sound like I'm doubting myself. But at the end of the day, the only thing that matters most is what kind of guy she would choose to be with.

I don't know what I'm lacking or how I should proceed in this chase. But still, I have a feeling in my heart that she would be mine. I would do anything for that. I pray to God to have her and be with me forever. This feeling of the chase that I'm currently experiencing is just quite amazing. In the end, it will solely be the Almighty's choice whether He wants me to suffer more pain or let me out of sorrow for the time being."

Yours,
Adam James"

As I read those lines, I began to suspect that Adam had fallen in love again, perhaps with someone he met during his youth. It struck me that he seemed like a guy who kept falling for one girl after another. I couldn't grasp the nature of this love. Even though his words were filled with depth and emotion, I felt like I was missing something about what was going on in his mind.

Marie looked up from the diary, sensing my confusion. "It sounds like Adam was deeply in love again, doesn't it?" she asked.

I nodded, still puzzled. "Yeah, it does. But it also feels like he's just moving from one infatuation to another. I can't quite figure out what kind of love this is."

Marie frowned, thinking. "It's strange. His writing is so passionate and intense. He clearly felt something profound, but it's hard to understand his exact feelings."

I sighed, feeling frustrated. "Exactly. It seems like with each passing day, he was falling for her more and more. It was like love at first sight, but then everything that followed was filled with art, music, and prose. He was more passionate about those things than ever."

Marie smiled softly. "Maybe that's just how he experienced love. Through art and music, expressing his feelings in a way that words alone couldn't capture."

I leaned back, considering her words. "Maybe. But it's still hard to grasp. It's like there's a piece of the puzzle missing, something that would make it all make sense."

Marie nodded in agreement. "I guess some things are just meant to remain a mystery."

With that, we both fell silent, each lost in our thoughts about Adam's enigmatic love story.

"*February 3, 2015*

Dear Alex,

I have been waiting for weeks, longing to know when she might return. How much longer must I endure this sadness and the faint hope that one day, you will come back?

Yours,

Adam James
"

"February 6, 2015

Dear Alex,

I finally understood something today: I may appear strong, having managed to live all these years on my own, but the reality is I am quite fragile. Heartbreaks and the need for affection take me a long time to recover from. When I went through something bad, I thought I could sustain myself through it all, but the truth is, I struggled deeply. I couldn't sustain the weight of that emotional break.

I've realized that I don't really know how to process or cope with these intense emotions. I always believed I was resilient, but now I see that I'm more vulnerable than I ever admitted to myself. This vulnerability feels like a crack in my armor, a part of me that I've tried to ignore but can no longer deny.

Now, I need to figure out a way to navigate through this. I need to find a way to understand and heal from these emotional wounds. It's clear that I can't keep pretending to be invincible. I have to face these feelings head-on, no matter how painful it might be.

Yours,

Adam James

"

"February 10, 2015

Dear Alex,

I finally think it's time to give up on the chase. It feels like a waste of my resources and time, and I'm not sure I'd be satisfied even if I succeeded.

Rather than losing myself in this pursuit, draining my feelings, energy, and emotions, I think it's better to focus on building myself up and stopping the chase. Instead of waiting for you to say "No" to me, I should be the one to step back.

I might say something like, "Your obsession makes me feel like I can't compete or make you mine. So, I'm sorry, but I can't keep chasing you or putting in the effort for you. I hope you find someone who meets your needs. At first, I thought you were different from the crowd, but it turns out you're just like everyone else."

See ya, Alex. Life is full of mysteries, and maybe being good isn't worth it after all.
Yours,
Adam James
"

"February 14, 2015
Dear Alex,

Please reply to people, whether it's an offensive remark or a simple statement, considering their time. What I value most is time. Sometimes, I think that if I had invested some time in getting to know you, we might have been better off as friends—or maybe even as something more. But now, I'm not so sure.

I do care about you. I think I might understand you a bit, but instead of chasing you, watching your Instagram, and waiting for replies that never come, it sucks. I don't know if you're doing it to test me, make fun of me, or if it's due to social awkwardness or family obligations. Whatever the reason, just tell me. It's painful and frustrating to see you not replying for days.

I fell for your shyness and loneliness. I thought I might be able to change that, but it takes effort from both sides. "A single hand can't clap."

If I bother you, just say, "No, I don't like you," or "I'm not interested, don't bother me." I have learned the discipline, so I won't dare bother you if you're clear. A simple "No, don't bother me" is enough. Initially, it might be heartbreaking, but I've experienced this pain in my life. It slowly fades, though it never completely goes away.

So please, in the name of God, speak up, sis. I pray you find someone you like. But don't play with my emotions if I don't matter to you.

Please don't toy with human emotions. I'm quite fragile. I have gone through a lot, and I've been slowly recovering. So please, let me go. I don't think you can support me if you can't even reply.

I won't say any bad words, but just go find someone to love. I enjoyed our one-sided silent talks, like old-time pigeon messengers. That's all from my side.

Yours,

Adam James"

"**February 17, 2015**

Dear Alex,

Yesterday was a day of frustration, but today brings a wiser understanding of things I had previously misunderstood, even while considering *myself a rational thinker.*

Another important lesson is learning to accept and be prepared for the possibility of worse. We need to start managing feelings of jealousy. This girl I'm thinking of has been teaching me this, though it's also what frustrates me the most—her ignorance. I need to learn to address the anger caused by being ignored, a lesson not easily learned over years of controlling immense frustration.

Whether or not I end up with her, I will always be grateful for how she has helped me gain control over my anger and frustration. She has taught me the importance of evolving.

I won't waste another page on this, for the chapter is over.

Yours,

Adam James "

" **February 20, 2015**

Dear Alex,

From this day forward, I am determined to let go of the past and embrace a new beginning. A rebirth of sorts, where I can leave behind what no longer serves me.

The one motivational line that has sustained me through it all is: "Everything happens for our own good." Even when faced with adversity, I hold on to the belief that these challenges are merely stepping stones, paving the way for something brighter and better.

Yours,

Adam James

"

"February 23, 2015
Dear Alex,

I've been thinking a lot about living with a true purpose in life. Without a purpose, our life feels worthless. I need something more, something achievable.

Talking about my daily experiences, it feels good when there's not much pressure on my head. You can shine like a bright star. I don't know when I started thinking this way, but I've come to realize that I need to see myself as more capable than anyone else.

During a casual conversation with a friend, he questioned me, implying that I was merely parroting ideas rather than creating something original. This struck a nerve, and as we conversed, I was determined to prove the authenticity of my work. In doing so, I discovered a complexity within myself—a realization that I must focus on myself rather than chasing meaningless pursuits.

One more thing, though not particularly good, happened today. I expressed some nonsense and let my feelings out in front of someone I shouldn't have. I sometimes feel that this shouldn't have happened. More than anything, I'm looking to redefine myself and start progressing in that direction.

Yours,
*Adam James***"**

"February 27, 2015
Dear Alex,

Now that my mind has returned to its usual state, clarity has dawned upon me. I recognize that the fault lay with me during my conversation with one of my friends, yesterday about the nature of boys and their approach to dating. Often, they seek merely a date, not genuine friendship. I have come to understand that one must be well aware of the fantasies that occupy our minds. We boys often conjure numerous scenarios when a girl speaks kindly and initiates conversation. However, we seldom take the time to comprehend her true feelings, especially when she is not interested in anything beyond friendship.

This realization has broadened my perspective. It has become evident to me that it is not always necessary to propose to someone you admire. Instead, you can cherish the bond of friendship, perhaps even cultivate a close or best friendship, without ever jeopardizing that precious connection.
Yours,
Adam James"

"March 3, 2015
Dear Alex,
It all started when I passed through the door, feeling bored and anxious. The rejection I faced recently had left an unconscious shadow over me, and I couldn't shake the bad feelings. I wondered if I would ever find someone like her again. But as they say, everything happens for our own good, whether it be pleasant or painful. Determined to overcome this, I decided to put an end to these feelings.

I realized that I needed to overcome the feeling of jealousy. Achieving what I desire might take a long time, or I might never achieve it at all. I began to doubt whether any girl would genuinely like me for who I am, fearing they might only be interested in what I can offer materially. Instead of chasing an elusive soulmate, I turned my focus to something else—something that could help me overcome this feeling of emptiness.

The concept of a soulmate, so beautifully portrayed in art, poetry, and music, often feels like an illusion. In reality, relationships don't last because of some mystical connection; they last because of commitment. Looks are important, as are finances, but mostly, it's about how you perceive the relationship. If you're looking for something casual, it's fine to approach it simply without thinking about commitments. But if you're serious, it's your duty to consider all aspects—commitment, finances, family, and more.

Thinking rationally is the only way to find something meaningful. Yet, I still crave something more, something crazy. I don't know if I could marry someone who hasn't achieved something extraordinary, someone not at my level. But despite these musings, life continues.

Yesterday, I returned to town. It was raining heavily, the city drenched and chaotic, mirroring my tumultuous feelings. My home, in those rainy days, remains my sanctuary. It is the holy land where I might find something I truly care about.
Yours,

Adam James"

"March 7, 2015
Dear Alex,

Today, I found myself wondering if I truly need someone in my life or if it's merely a delusion. I pondered this for a while and came to a conclusion that might foster my developmental goals. It all began with the notion of being "focused," as a girl once claimed. At first, I was irritated—if she is focusing on her life, then what am I doing? But thinking about it more rationally, I now feel she was correct in some way.

For someone like me, who always strives to be the best at everything, the journey to success is different. I'm not like the average guy, drifting aimlessly. Before chasing or getting the girl I want, I must first consider every kind of possible scenario.

So, chasing and looking for a soulmate should not be my primary goal. My primary goal should be to be myself, not the boy of some random girl.
Yours,
Adam James"

"March 15, 2015
Dear Alex,
Many days have passed since we last talked, and things have changed. I find myself unable to fall for anyone else. Instead, I am falling again for the same girl who rejected me the first time I fell in love with her. My feelings for that introverted girl once

filled me with anger and frustration as I tried to understand her behavioral patterns. But it all boils down to one thing: "It's natural." I finally understand that we, as men, are also lustful in a broader sense. It's natural that she hasn't fallen for someone yet; she comes from a conservative background and is socially awkward. Despite these traits, my intuition tells me she is a very good-hearted person. I see her at least once a day while crossing paths, and I can't help but be drawn to her.

Looking back, I sometimes feel that I should not have been so hasty in trying to make her mine. But that period was fraught with the sensation of losing love. It was hard, rough, and difficult. Yet, here I am, falling for her again. It's as if I want her in my life or no one else. It's either her or no one. Every night, I hopelessly pray to have her in my life at some point. Girls like her are very rare and becoming extinct day by day, and I want her. She is truly something special. Despite the differences between us, I am determined to try every possible means until the last day.

Sometimes, I feel like calling her. I want her to be my everything. I want her to gain my everything. I want her.

Yours,

Adam James
"

Marie fell asleep on my shoulder. Her face, so serene and beautiful, resembled that of a peaceful nine-year-old. I had never seen her like this before; she was so vulnerable and relaxed. Gently, I lifted her head from my shoulder and placed it softly on the bed, not wanting to disturb her deep sleep. She mumbled something incoherent, but her breathing soon returned to its slow, rhythmic pattern.

I turned back to the diary. The pages I had covered so far were a mix of various emotions, from the giddy excitement of love at first sight to the deep bond of friendship that had formed over time and the chaos that ensued along the way. It seemed like the author was flowing through time with his feelings, navigating through different phases of life with a raw and honest voice.

The short poems scattered throughout the diary were poignant and heartfelt, something I hadn't encountered in ages. Each one felt like a glimpse into the author's soul, revealing his innermost thoughts and emotions. I found myself deeply moved by his words.

My eyes began to trouble me, signaling that it was time to rest. I closed the diary, feeling a mix of emotions swirling inside me. There was still so much left to read, but the weight of the day was finally catching up to me. I placed the diary on the bedside table and turned off the lamp, casting the room into darkness.

As I lay down next to Marie, I couldn't help but think about the connections we form with others and the lasting impact they have on our lives.

With a final glance at Marie, who was now sound asleep, I closed my eyes and let myself drift off, knowing that I would return to the diary soon to uncover the rest of its secrets.

FIVE
THE LAST FALL

"**March 24, 2015**
Dear Alex,

Recently, I reconnected with an old friend, a girl I once had a crush on. We resolved our past conflicts and are now on good terms again. She was, after all, the first person I admire the most. She's stunningly beautiful, but I've realized I no longer harbor any romantic interest in her.

What's more significant is that my confidence has been steadily returning. I'm beginning to understand people better, which feels incredibly empowering. I'm happy to report that my "rebooting process" and transition into the friend zone with a certain someone might soon be complete. My feelings toward her have become more nuanced; while I see her potential as a life partner, her conservative nature and realistic demeanor sometimes clash with my desires.
Yours,
Adam James

"

As I read those lines, I grasped what was coming next. I felt ready to delve into the words on the pages. However, I decided not to involve Marie in this reading session. I got up and moved toward the seldom-visited room in our house. Taking the keys, I unlocked the door. The room was filled with dust, but my determination to complete the reading overshadowed any discomfort.

I cleaned a small space for myself, establishing a little reading nook. I grabbed a chair, leaned it against the wall, and settled in. With a deep breath, I started reading the entries that awaited me, ready to uncover more of Adam's thoughts and emotions.

"**March 25, 2015**

Dear Alex,

Today, I had the chance to reconnect with an old friend after such a long time. Remarkably, our conversation flowed as if the six years apart had never happened. We spoke with such ease and comfort that it felt like no time had passed. She was curious about how we could be so at ease with each other. I explained that I had been through a lot over the past two or three years—experiencing isolation and other challenges. This period of introspection and redefinition has allowed me to engage more meaningfully, which is why our conversation felt so natural and majestic.

Yours,

Adam James

"

"**March 29, 2015**

Hey Alex,

As everyday life starts, our working hours increase, and we must find our true time amidst our busyness to regain our composure. As I grow older, I strive to become the best in various fields. Day and night, my mind is consumed with the desire to excel. Soon, I will be the ultimate best version of myself.

My interest lies in exploring and learning new things. Romance seems less important now. My family, friends, and myself are all I need. If someone were to elaborate on the concept of marriage, I'd argue that paying others for care is more efficient. Marriage would only compromise my freedom.

I find solace in fine-tuning the rhythms of my piano. This girl has motivated me to be the best version of myself.

Lastly, there's someone who blocked me for six years. I only observed her from afar, but now she talks to me. I don't know why. She's beautiful and intelligent, an ideal life partner. But I want to develop a hatred for her because falling for her would be reckless. She won't be my friend, and I don't want that. She loves flirting, and I don't want to be a mere pawn in her game.

Yours,

Adam James"

"**April 4, 2015**

Dear Alex,

Something happened yesterday that shouldn't have happened. It was unexpected and stirred up a lot of emotions. Lacking emotional intelligence, I ended the conversation.

I didn't realize how much this incident would affect me. A slight desire to care for her emerged, which shouldn't have. She's my friend, and while she could become my best friend, I don't want to go beyond that. She deserves someone better. She's an incredible person, and If someday I might fall for her, I don't want to fall for her looks; I want to fall for who she is.

I want to see her grow from afar and be a good friend she can rely on in difficult times. I just want to cherish her and take care of her since she seems to have a childish, not-so-adult nature. She is adorable—only a little else to say.

Yours,

Adam James
"

"April 6, 2015

Dear Alex,

Today's story is an embarrassing one, but here it goes. Yesterday, I had a pleasant dream, yet filled with insecurities about how I would deal with them.

It started with me spending time with a friend from 8th grade. She was a good friend back then, but we hadn't talked for six years due to some misunderstanding. In my dream, we were enjoying each other's company. She was beautiful and simple, inside and out. I felt blessed to share time with her.

Things got more interesting as we became more than just friends. We explored places, ate food, and wandered everywhere. One day, our faces came closer while traveling in an autorickshaw together. It was a cold December, with fog and warmth of breath mixing. As we came closer, she held me by my arm, and we looked into each other's eyes. Her face looked the most gorgeous in the dark, with her shining white skin and sparkling eyes.

We both leaned in, and my lips pressed against her smooth cheek, sliding to the border of her reddish-pink lips. I hesitated, feeling I might have done something wrong, but she pulled me closer by my neck, deepening the kiss. We were immersed in the heat of the moment, just feeling each other. My tongue moved inside her mouth, feeling the softness of her tongue, making the kiss more intense. It felt like this moment would last forever, but soon, our destination arrived, and we had to get off at our stops.

But I don't know what happened next. But her companionship always felt like an honor to me.
Yours,
Adam James
"

*"***April 12, 2015**
Hey Alex,

Long time no see! So, some dramatic things have happened this year so far.

Now, returning to my friend, I still don't know if I have profound feelings for her or if I just want to be true to myself and stay the way I am until I truly fall for someone. May our friendship never break,

and may we enjoy each other's company as friends, lovers, or more throughout our lives.
Yours,
Adam James
"

"**April 17, 2015**
Hey Alex,

Today, I wanted to tell you about my ambition and my journey of wanting more and more. I've realized that I am constantly asking for more, and there is no satisfaction. Life is full of insecurities, and I always want to achieve more to prove myself, though I don't know to whom. I'm just insecure and aiming mindlessly, nevertheless.

There are numerous things I want to achieve in life. I don't know why, but I just want to be the best at everything I do.
Yours,
Adam James
"

"**April 21, 2015**
Dear Alex,

Hey bro! I wanted to share something interesting with you today. Yesterday, I had a long conversation with her. I apologized to her, and we've been talking again since then. So, on Sunday, while I was working, I called her. We ended up talking about a lot of things afterward, ranging from life and relationships to various other topics.

Our conversation lasted for three straight hours, the longest conversation I've ever had. To my surprise, it didn't feel like I was talking to someone unknown or just a girl; it felt as comfortable as talking to a close male friend. One particular question she asked me was, "What would you do if someone approached you?" I was taken aback and sensibly replied, "I don't know. I don't know how I'll react, but one thing is for sure: I won't accept anything until I figure out what I am going to do in life." It might take time, and I might miss out on many things, but that's not my focus right now. I just want to explore and live my life to the fullest.

I don't want to waste time thinking about what others think of me. I don't want to pursue anything forcefully. I want to be the master of myself, not a slave to others. I want to learn and explore.

During our conversation, I also discovered something interesting: girls feel shy when topics like having kids are brought up. That was a new finding for me.
Yours,
Adam James
"

"**April 27, 2015**
Dear Alex,

Today is the day, and it has me reflecting on the passage of time and the constancy of certain things. I feel like years will pass, and everything will stay the same. I'll remain my own support and source of happiness, not relying on anyone else. Everyone else will be there, but I'll truly be living for myself.

Sometimes, I find that being self-centered helps me a lot. It shields me from the harms of the outer world. Not having someone to love might be one of the best things because it allows me to focus on my own progress and fulfill my needs.

One important thing I need to remember is to stop caring about what others say or do to me. At the end of the day, it's me that matters most.
Yours,
Adam James
"

"May 2, 2015
Hey Alex,

Interestingly, a girl who once had a crush on me attended the event. It seemed as if she wanted to approach me, as she made an effort to talk. While it's nice, But I'm not ready for a relationship at this point.

Despite these thoughts, I recognize my uncertainty about relationships. I don't want to make half-hearted decisions about choosing a partner. I long for someone who has known me since childhood, someone who understands me inside and out, someone who can sustain and keep me grounded. Such a person, however, seems to be a rarity, which is why I remain alone, perhaps for life.
Yours,
Adam James
"

"**May 7, 2015**

Hey Alex,

Yesterday, I had a deep conversation with one of my friends about my experiences in Life. She believes I possess a unique personality, something special, though I remain unsure of myself and my emotions. In this state of uncertainty and confusion, I think it is wise to place my trust in time and let it reveal what the future holds.
Yours,
Adam James
"

"**May 11, 2015**

Dear Alex,

I've been thinking more and more about that one friend—conversations and things I want to discuss with her keep popping into my mind. I believe I have feelings for her, but then I start thinking I don't and that I shouldn't chase her. It's difficult. I rationalize everything a lot, spending a lot of time thinking before making bold decisions. My confused state of mind prevents me from making any bold decisions right now. Maybe I'll be too late, and she'll go for someone else. I don't know what will happen. Only time will tell what the future holds for me and her. It'll be interesting to see, and I should prepare myself for any consequences.

A few days ago, I talked with Marie about what she's currently doing and how her life is going. We discussed life before and after. We talked about potential conflicts and how they might deal with

them. Listening to her, I believe I'm in a better situation living by myself. She also mentioned something, saying that if I were in a relationship, I'd understand and think about these things more thoroughly. But I explained calmly that I'm currently figuring out what I want to pursue and that I'm not interested in any relationships at the moment.
Yours,
Adam James
"

"**May 14, 2015**
Hey Alex,

I've reached a conclusion regarding my personal relationships. I've realized that playing it safe and delaying my feelings for the sake of pursuing something greater and all the other steps might be a distraction rather than a genuine interest.

I now feel that the person with whom I feel most compatible needs to know that I am developing feelings for her, regardless of the potential consequences. Though I'm still uncertain about myself, I am somewhat confident. I believe I should not delay any longer and find a way to express my feelings or at least validate them with someone close to her. It's a risk I need to take to stabilize my mind.

I've been reflecting on our last conversation, and it has led me to the realization that I have fallen for her. Despite my uncertainties, I feel compelled to seek your advice. Should I first clarify my path and then express my feelings, or should I directly

convey my emotions, bypassing other concerns, to see if she would support me in difficult times? Or am I overthinking? Lastly, do you think she might perceive me as just another guy, no different from the rest?
Yours,
Adam James
"

"**May 20, 2015**
Hey Alex,

The instability within my mind, I don't know whether a result of rationality or burgeoning wisdom, constantly navigates from east to west, north to south, seeking clarity on my true feelings for her. Each passing day adds layers of complexity to this inner struggle. At the sight of her or a glimpse of her presence, nerves spiral, yet amidst conversation, a semblance of ease emerges, allowing for more fluid communication on various topics.

I often keep myself and my mind simulating in hypothetical scenarios, contemplating how I would react if she were to find companionship or marry someone else. I consciously try to guide my thoughts to a positive outlook, reassuring myself that such circumstances should not lead to despair and rat,her I should be happy and stay as positive as I can. It occurs to me now that mentally simulating these potential life events may indeed equip us to navigate them with grace if they were to manifest in reality.
Yours,
Adam James

"

"**May 24, 2015**

Hey Alex,

Today, a sense of loss lingers within me. I had hoped to initiate our conversation with a touch of humor or a flirtatious vibe, yet it didn't unfold as anticipated. Yesterday, I playfully texted a close old friend. However, her response was a simple "Thanks a lot!" which left me feeling that perhaps she's growing weary of our conversations, lacking interest in further dialogue. I'm unsure of the reason behind this shift, but I sense it's time to put things to the test—to cease messaging her and refrain from inconveniencing her any further.

It's possible that recent conversations or the current situation may have left an impression, perhaps portraying me in a light she perceives as less desirable, leading her to distance herself from our exchanges. I can't fully fathom my emotions to arrive at a conclusion, but I fear that when clarity dawns, it may already be too late—she may have found her partner or chosen a different path. As for me, I may continue my journey in solitude. May her future be radiant, filled with happiness and love with whomever she may choose.

I was born and raised as a loner, navigating life's traumas and adult experiences, grappling with the loss of loved ones during crucial years, all while yearning for someone to lean on. This solitude seems destined to be my companion as I move forward, a loner amidst a world of companionship and

flourishing love stories.
Yours,
Adam James
"

"**May 27, 2015**
Hey Alex,

What are these intricate feelings I have for her? I struggle to comprehend if it's love, a longing for her companionship, or perhaps something entirely different. Lately, these emotions have become a daily occurrence: her face greeting me as I awaken, her conversations echoing in my mind during the day, and a strong desire to chat with her lingering before I drift into sleep. Yet, the true nature of my feelings remains elusive. Is it love? Is it companionship? Is it something more profound?

Whatever it may be, I sense a subtle shift within my heart. It's as if she, or memories of her, are finding a place to reside once again in the chambers of my heart. She was my first crush, my initial true friend with whom I deeply resonated. She holds a significant place in my life—a vital piece of my existence. I ponder whether I would find contentment in solitude, adhering strictly to my ideals, or if her companionship is the key to enduring happiness amidst the challenges that lie ahead.

Regardless, she will always be my closest confidante, cherished as my best pal from my perspective. Should our friendship evolve into something more, I envision cherishing that moment and endeavoring to bring her the utmost joy in life.

Yours,
Adam James
"

"June 2, 2015
Hey Alex,

It's been three days of discomfort, my heartbeat racing uncontrollably. I find myself losing focus and control at this crucial juncture. My thoughts are consumed by her, our conversations endlessly replaying in my mind, gnawing away at my peace.

Our dialogues were eerily synchronized. When I spoke of my desire to explore the world, she echoed the same yearning. I praised art and philosophy as noble pursuits, and she concurred with equal fervor. On the topic of relationships, I mentioned my inclination toward solitude and self-discovery. She inquired what I would do if approached by a girl, and I candidly replied that I was still figuring out my life's purpose. Until I do, I can't imagine entering a relationship for fear of dragging someone else down with me if I fail.

I have come to realize that "like attracts like." Despite our differences, we share numerous similarities. I have flirted and engaged deeply with several women, though only one became my girlfriend. Similarly, she has navigated the modern world with many friends and admirers, including accomplished suitors. Recklessly falling for her seems unlikely to win her over. If she desires someone, it will be because she genuinely wants them.

Thus, I believe the chances of her falling for me are slim. Nevertheless, once I have figured out my own path, I would be glad to express my feelings to her, regardless of the outcome.
Yours,
Adam James
"

"**June 6, 2015**
Hey Alex,

Oh, why on earth do I keep getting visions of her? Every time my mind wanders, her voice breezes through my ears—the sweet, childish tone combined with her charming personality melts my heart as if it were an ice cube, and her aura is the warmth causing it to melt. She is so wondrous and unique that finding someone like her would take years, if ever.

Today, I found it very difficult to sleep. I tried falling asleep at 2 AM but didn't manage to until 5 AM. My mind was filled with random thoughts of her, and I found myself smiling and blushing at the hallucinations of her. Could it be that I have truly fallen in love? Yet, I don't want to do anything about it. I am content with our friendship—nothing more, nothing less.

Today, I had an important dream, or perhaps it was another vision of her. It began in a beautiful place full of greenery, trees, and high mountains. A cold breeze filled the atmosphere, evoking a cherry blossom-like feeling. We were holding each other's hands and moving forward in time. Slowly, we grew closer and sat side by side at a table, feeling warmth, love, and affection more profound than anything else in the universe. My hand moved through her hair, dispersing her golden strands to the side, some falling on my shoulder, filling my face with the sensation of passion. My lips touched the side of her neck, and in those moments, I felt engulfed in emotion, my mind going blank, losing all control over myself.

Yours,

Adam James
"

"*June 9, 2015*

Hey Alex,

My mind is constantly buzzing with thoughts about various aspects of my life. I've navigated through bad times to good times, and this transition is nothing short of amazing, teaching me so much along the way.

As I grow older, I find myself reflecting more deeply on my life and its future possibilities. I think about building my own path and chasing my dreams, as well as what my personal love life might look like if it ever materializes. There's this one thing I find particularly challenging—falling for someone regardless of their past.

However, I'm still uncertain about my true feelings for her and whether she remains the girl with the morals and values I once admired. I'm unsure about many things if I were to enter a relationship with her. I often feel like I overthink everything, but I want to stay true to myself and make decisions that I won't regret. At the same time, I need to see if our conversations are just friendly or something more.

In chasing my dreams and striving to reach the highest possible stature, I feel like I'm losing out on the personal side of life—my family, my time, and my relationships. These things have stopped making sense or exciting me. Grinding, enduring pain, and building something great to make a personal and social impact are what keep me going. This pursuit excites me more than anything else. Building something brings me immense pleasure, no matter how difficult it is.

But what if I lose the one person I feel most comfortable with, the one I imagine as my life companion, to someone else? It might feel bad until I find someone I resonate with on a deep level. Ideally, it would be someone who has seen me grow from childhood, understands who I am, and shares a deep trust and connection with me. My heart no longer beats the way it used to when I felt something special for someone. Still, I wrote this poem:

It was my first time meeting you,
A new girl, you changed your class,
Intelligent, sweet, and beautiful with values,
Too good, too perfect, like a goddess!
Slowly, chatting and gossiping with you,
I started developing feelings, still ignoring you.
Once, it led to six years of no talk.

She was so naive. But I don't know what the future holds for her and me.
Yours,

Adam James"

"

June 12, 2015

Hey!

I wanted to share a recent experience that left me feeling uneasy. The first dream involved someone I believe I have feelings for—an old friend. The details of the setting are hazy, but the events unfolded as follows: we were having a conversation when, quite suddenly, things took an unexpected turn. She asked me how long I intended to make her wait, implying that if I delayed any longer, she might accept a proposal from someone else. She was insistent that I propose to her right then and there. Otherwise, she might stop waiting for me. Her eagerness to enter a relationship was palpable, while I felt uncertain. Despite my hesitation, I proposed.

My heart raced, and even now, as I recount the dream, I can feel it pounding. In the dream, we walked together and eventually entered an empty classroom. I felt incredibly awkward, and then she grabbed me, romanticizing the moment. It struck me that this is what happens when one holds back for so many years. There were more moments where she took control of the situation, and although I didn't mind, it was a bit frightening.

Yours,

Adam James
"

"*June 15, 2015*

Dear Alex,

This morning, I awoke from a dream that set my heart racing, evoking a mix of emotions—some pleasant, others not so. The dream was both vivid and elusive. It began with a reunion of our class, but we were older, no longer the youthful selves we are now. Chaos ensued as people shouted and engaged in random antics. Amidst the disorder, I assumed the role of a leader, calming everyone and guiding the class forward.

In another scene, I found myself entangled in a conflict over space, displaying a more egotistical side. As the class concluded, the girl I liked stood at the door, her hand extended, inviting me to join her. In my foolishness, I failed to understand her gesture and merely asked, "What?" Embarrassed, she withdrew her hand and left. It was only after she had gone, as I gathered my belongings that I realized the significance of her gesture, but by then, it was too late to find her again.

To Her,

Yesterday, I dreamt of you once more, and it wasn't the first time. Despite my avowed disinterest in girls, it seems I've fallen for you. My heart races, and I long to spend more time with you.

Thought:

When we first met, it seemed inconsequential, but I found in you a kindred spirit with whom I could connect on every level—intellectual, comical, and more. Our time together became increasingly enjoyable, surpassing anything I had experienced before. You never complained or retaliated, no matter how ridiculous my jokes or actions were. But our friendship faltered due to my misbehavior and negligence, leading to a painful separation. Those six years were bleak, as I had lost a close friend through my own fault.

However, time healed the wounds. My third apology finally mended our relationship, and since then, our friendship has flourished anew. It feels as though two lost souls have been reunited.
Yours,
Adam James
"

"*June 18, 2015*
Hey Alex,

Reflecting on my love life, I find myself once again drawn to someone—the very same person for whom I first fell years ago. Despite my efforts to convince myself otherwise, I can't help but feel that familiar spark reigniting. I fear she might see me as just another admirer, no different from the rest.

I am uncertain where this path will lead, but I know that missing the chance to express my feelings would leave me with regret. Regardless of the outcome, I must convey my emotions to her. With each passing day, I feel an increasing attachment, a growing addiction to her presence.

This period of uncertainty leaves me longing for her support and love, believing that her companionship would fill the void in my life, bringing fulfillment and satisfaction. Without her,

I feel trapped in an endless race, striving to prove myself—to whom I do not even know. The desire for her love consumes my thoughts, and I am left yearning for a future where she is by my side.
Yours,
Adam James
"

"*June 24, 2015*

Hey Alex,

With each passing day, my heart beats more fervently for her. I feel myself falling deeper in love, yet uncertainty clouds my thoughts. I fear she may not reciprocate my feelings or, worse, might stop speaking to me if I reveal my true emotions. Once, in a conversation about why I mostly talked to her and Gauri, I candidly admitted that I had a crush on her. There was a tense silence for a few seconds before I quickly added that I was just a kid then, and the conversation resumed as normal.

Now, I yearn for her as my life partner more than anything else. I want to cherish every moment with her, sharing a life together filled with love and joy.
Yours,
Adam James
"

"*June 27, 2015*

Hey Alex,

Today, I don't know what happened to me. I can't quite grasp what's happening to me. It feels as though I'm still foolish and have yet to achieve wisdom in handling emotions. It's tough, it's difficult. Sometimes, it feels like this is the price I pay for having a chaotic mind filled with high-order thinking and wisdom. In this battle, my shortcomings have taken a significant toll on me.

Today, I received a text from her. She wanted to ask me something about the relationship status of our mutual friend's relationship. At first, I was shocked, a bit sad, and slightly depressed. A wave of bad feelings washed over me; I don't know what, I don't know how. This was the same feeling I felt every time when I was at the lowest points in my emotional cycle. My initial reaction was to preserve myself, convincing myself that I don't care and that I don't feel bad or sad about it. And I kept repeating to myself, "Everything happens for our own good."

Despite my efforts to protect myself, much more came out than I intended. I don't know what consequences this might have, but now I feel like I have nothing left. My true nature, or perhaps the darker side of me, was exposed. I was overwhelmed by emotions and expressed a lot more than I should have. Until now, I always believed that if a girl talks to you nicely, it doesn't necessarily mean she's interested in you. I've realized that even if she shares and tells you a lot, it doesn't mean she will fall for you.

I can't shake off the feeling that I was pranked or played by her. It's a terrible feeling. Somehow, the path I'm on and the events unfolding make me feel like my life stands on the pillars of sacrifices, giving up on things and becoming emotionally numb.
Yours,

Adam James
"

"June 27, 2015
Later Today,
Hey Alex!

I don't know why on earth my destiny is having erratic twists and turns. The conversation I had with her over the past 24 hours felt like a never-ending circular trail, moving back and forth without any clear direction. Sometimes, it seemed like things were progressing in one direction, only to abruptly twist and take a completely different turn. Perhaps I was a fool, caught in this spiraling trap.

Now, I am not getting what was with the casual talks the jokes, which were fine. But the flirtatious talk that reached an entirely new level of intrigue. It was hard to differentiate between what's real and what's fake. Despite expressing my feelings this morning and now facing the results by evening, I can't help but feel that girls are highly manipulative. It felt as if I was defeated, as if she had conquered me, proving that even I could fall for someone. Yet, as I state my thoughts now, I can't predict what the next second or minute will bring.

If, after a long time, something were to happen, I would most likely reject it. At this moment, I find myself caught in a confusing loop of if-else scenarios. Still, uncertainty lingers. I don't know what lies ahead, but perhaps my destiny holds a completely different path.
Yours,

Adam James"

*"**June 28, 2015***

Hey Alex!

Finally, everything has come to an end with all discussion, conclusion, clearing of thoughts, and exchange of ideas. I somehow feel I am not made for relationships. The last girl I decided to approach, after which I swore I would stop pursuing anyone, has turned me down. I was not able to handle my feelings properly. The pain is almost unbearable. It fucking blows my mind and heart. Although I know time will eventually heal these wounds, and I will find the strength to move forward. Life is troublesome, and I need a break.

This sensation in my chest is excruciating, and it's making it impossible for me to focus on anything else.

If these rejections had only affected me mentally, I might have been able to shrug them off. But when they touch my emotions internally and so deeply, it becomes almost unbearable. The future feels uncertain, and now I realize that my primary focus should be on myself. I can no longer allow myself to fall in love with anyone. But this is the end to it, and she was "THE LAST ONE."

Yours,

Adam James"

THE END

www.ingramcontent.com/pod-product-compliance
Lightning Source LLC
Chambersburg PA
CBHW031756150726
47989CB00006B/2750